W9-CFB-477

THE
LATE HIT

GRIDIRON

THE LATE HIT

K.R. COLEMAN

darby creek

MINNEAPOLIS

Darby Creek
A division of Lerner Publishing Group, Inc.
241 First Avenue North
Minneapolis, MN 55401 USA

For reading levels and more information, look up this title at
www.lernerbooks.com.

The images in this book are used with the permission of: © pattern line/Shutterstock.com (scratch texture); © Eky Studio/Shutterstock.com (metal bolts); © Kriangsak Osvapoositkul/Shutterstock.com (rust texture); © Volodymyr Melnyk/Dreamstime.com (players in stadium).

Main body text set in Janson Text LT Std 12/17.5.
Typeface provided by Adobe Systems.

Library of Congress Cataloging-in-Publication Data

The Cataloging-in-Publication Data for *The Late Hit* is on file at the Library of Congress.
ISBN 978-1-5124-3982-3 (lib. bdg.)
ISBN 978-1-5124-5352-2 (pbk.)
ISBN 978-1-5124-4871-9 (EB pdf)

Manufactured in the United States of America
1-42231-25780-1/4/2017

This book is dedicated to number 50 on the Solomon Gorillas football team.

Chapter

1

Anton and I are the first ones out on the field for practice. It's one of those perfect October days. The air is cool. The maple trees are lit up—orange and red and yellow against a bright blue sky. I've waited all day to get out on this field. I'm not good at sitting still in a classroom. I'm at my best when I'm moving around and forced to think on the fly.

Anton and I throw a football back and forth while we wait for the others to come out. I can tell his mind is somewhere else, but even though he's only half concentrating, he still throws a perfect spiral. It lands right in my hands.

I throw the ball back, but I don't have an arm

like his. No one on our team does. He's the best QB the Warren High Wolves have had in years, and the kid didn't even know a thing about football until we became friends in the fifth grade.

Anton was new to our school that year. His family moved to Warren because back then the mines were still open and paying well. I remember at recess how he used to just stand against a chain-link fence and watch the rest of us play touch football on the asphalt parking lot.

One day I threw him the football and told him to join the game, but he just tossed the ball back, shook his head, and walked off.

"You should play," I told him later as we were heading up the stairs to our classroom. I felt bad for him, standing there alone.

"I don't know how," he mumbled looking down at his feet as we headed down a hallway. "I've never played before."

"What?" I was stunned. "You have to learn!" Even back then, I loved everything about football. Watching it. Playing it.

Reading about it in the paper.

I invited Anton over to my house that Sunday to watch the Packers game. Afterward we went out back and my dad and I taught Anton how to throw and run the ball. He has come over to my house every Sunday since. We'll watch football on TV or play our own game in my backyard. It didn't take long for Anton to develop the best arm at our school. Soon he was the player everyone wanted on their team at recess.

"The Titans have some big defenders," I say, trying to pull Anton out of his own thoughts. Usually he's talkative and upbeat— excited about the upcoming game.

"Busby," Anton says, throwing the ball hard and fast. "We can't lose this game."

"I know," I say, catching it against my chest, surprised by the intensity of the throw. "It's a big game. We win, we go onto playoffs. We lose, our season is done. But we can beat the Titans. We have a better passing game."

"You don't understand. We *have* to win this," Anton says moving across the white lines toward me. When he is a few feet away, he looks back at the doors to the school to see if Coach has come out, then says: "The school board is thinking about closing down Warren High."

I think he's joking, but then I see his face. He's not making this up.

Chapter 2

"What?!" I feel like I've just taken a hit by a linebacker twice my size. I don't understand.

"I heard Ms. Jenkins and Mr. Leonard talking about it after school. They didn't know Ciara and I were standing outside the door."

"Why were you with Ciara?" I ask, distracted by the thought of her, but trying to sound casual. Anton knows I've had a crush on Ciara Johnson for years—I've never been good at hiding anything from him.

"Dude!" Anton looks at me, shaking his head. "Ciara and I both had to make up a quiz, but that's not the important part of this story.

Didn't you just hear me? They want to close down our school!"

"Right," I say, getting back on topic. "Why? Why do they want to do that?" I look past the goal posts and up at our school. The red brick building sits on top of a hill. It isn't a great school, but it isn't bad. My parents went here and my grandfather too. It has withstood a fire and a century of harsh winters. It's an anchor in this town. I may not love school, but I can't imagine going anywhere else.

"The school needs too many repairs," Anton says. "And there isn't any money in this town to fix it up—not since everybody lost their jobs at the mine."

Three years ago the iron ore mines just outside of town shut down. The company keeps saying they'll reopen, but they haven't. There are a lot of families struggling to make ends meet. My dad left to work in the oil fields until the mines reopen. It's a twelve-hour drive from here, and he lives in camper attached to the back of his truck. We only see him one weekend a month. He says it's just temporary—that it's just a matter of time before the mines reopen—but it's been over a year now.

I hold the football tightly between my two hands.

"They're just going to close it down? What are we going to do next year? Our senior year? Where are we supposed to go?"

Anton kneels down to tie his cleat.

"I heard Ms. Jenkins say half of us will be sent to Caulfield High and the other half to Pine Falls."

"Send us to different schools? Split us all up?" The words tumble hard and fast out of my mouth. Thoughts of having to spend my senior year at either one of those schools make me feel sick. I can't imagine walking down a hallway and not seeing half the faces I know—faces like Anton's and Ciara's.

The rest of our team comes out on the field.

"What about the Wolves? What about Coach Quimbley?" I ask.

Anton shakes his head. "This could be it for the Wolves."

Chapter 3

Out of frustration and anger, I throw the ball at the stands and hear it hit the wooden stairs. There's a strange hollow echo. I stand there for a moment realizing that there might not even be a place for me on another team. I'm not huge. I'm only five foot ten and lanky for a fullback, but Coach likes how I play. He's put a lot of faith in me this year, and I'm only as good as I am because of his coaching.

"What if we're at different schools? On different teams?" I ask Anton.

His face becomes hard. The two of us have played on the same line since our freshman year, and before that we were always on the same team—even during our elementary school recess games. I've made it my main focus to protect Anton out on the field. It was the only way that we could get Anton's mom to sign the forms to let him play football in the first place. I promised his mom that I'd watch out for him. And so far I've kept my word.

Coach comes out on the field. He's wearing a blue and silver baseball hat and matching shirt. He walks to the center of the field where the rest of the team starts to gather around.

"We can't let them break up this team. We can't let them just close our school," I whisper to Anton.

"Nothing has been decided yet. The board still needs to vote," Anton says as he walks with me to the stands to retrieve the ball I've thrown up there. "If we win and keep winning—if the whole town is cheering us on, it'll be hard for them to close our school."

"What if winning isn't enough?" I ask.

"There's been too much loss in this town. We need to win," Anton says with finality.

"We will win."

I climb over the small metal fence and into the stands. I want to believe like Anton does—believe that a win will save our school. But I know the roof leaks, and last winter the boiler broke down three times. It was so cold inside, we all wore our coats and hats to class, but it was also fun. It was one of those experiences that could only happen at Warren High, and we look back on it with pride.

My cleats clunk up the white, wooden staircase. I find the football in the third row, and when I reach down to pick it up, I see all the names carved into the bleachers. The names have been painted over, but they're still clearly visible. Letters etched so deeply in the wood that no amount of paint could cover them up fully. My dad's name is on one of these benches. He showed it to me once. My grandfather's name is here too. It's something all the seniors do when they graduate from Warren High—find a bench and carve their name in it, letting the world know they were a part of Warren history.

I trace over some letters and wonder if I'll ever get a chance to carve my name alongside the rest. What will happen to these stands? To this field? To these names? We can't let this be the end.

"Busby! What are you doing up there? Get over here," Coach yells at me.

I hold up the ball for him to see. It feels heavier than it did before. It feels for a moment as if it's filled with sand. I head down the stairs and over the fence. Anton and I walk towards the fifty yard line where everyone else is gathered.

Chapter

4

Coach motions for the team to take a knee, and we all look up at him. I can see in his face that he's heard about the possibility of Warren High closing too. His jaw is tight as he chomps down on a piece of cinnamon gum, and there's a deep crease across his forehead.

He holds up two fingers.

"Two days to get ready," Coach says. "Two days to prepare. Two days to work on efficiency and focus and speed. The Titans might be a bigger team, with a deeper bench, but we have played this season like a well-oiled machine. And that's how we'll win. We are going to be flawless out there. No mistakes."

"No mistakes!" we all shout back.

Then Anton stands up and looks at Coach. At six foot two, he's nearly as tall as Coach, but he's not as wide.

Anton takes off his helmet and holds it in his hands. "Coach, are they thinking of closing Warren High down?"

The rest of the team starts talking all at once. A bunch of us stand up. Coach chews on his gum for a few seconds too long. Then holds up his hands and doesn't say a thing until we are quiet again and down on one knee.

"That's all just talk," he says and then looks at each of us. "And we can't let this talk break our focus. We need to concentrate on beating the Titans. We can't focus on something that isn't clear. Focus on now. Focus on here. Focus on how to win Friday night."

"But we need to know," Anton pushes. "Is it true? Will there be a vote?"

Coach takes off his baseball hat and runs his fingers through his short hair.

"Enough," he says. "We can practice and work hard or talk about rumors and gossip."

"If the board is thinking about closing down our school . . ." Anton starts. I can tell he's about to give a speech about how a win could change the school board's mind, but Coach cuts him off.

"Run the stairs," Coach points to the stands.

I watch Anton turn around, but I have his back. I've always had his back. I stand up and say what he wanted to say: "That's why we have to play like we've never played before. We have to make this town care about our school. If they have pride in us, in this school, they aren't going to let the board shut us down."

Coach looks at me and is quiet for a moment. That was the most I've ever said in front of this team. I'm not one of the guys that gives pep talks; I usually keep my head down.

"Busby," he says slowly. "Nice speech. Now you can join Anton and run the stairs. Fifty times. Up and down. Now. Go."

Anton and I head to the bleachers.

"He knows we're right," Anton says.

I nod at this. The two of us make a good team—I have no idea what I'll do if we're split up.

"We're going to win," Anton says. "We can't just let the Wolves go down without a fight. We need to keep playing for as long as we can."

Chapter 5

We run up and down the stairs. At the top, I touch a few names on a bench. I don't know the faces these names belong to, but I know that we have to win on Friday for them too.

My legs burn when we are done. We head back over to where the rest of the team is lined up to practice, but Coach won't let us take the field. He calls the two of us over to the sideline where he's standing.

"No more interruptions!" He yells at us. "Focus! Focus on what is happening right here. Right now." And then he lowers his voice, looks at both of us, and says, "I'm depending on both of you to lead this team to victory. Do you understand? Be leaders out there. Not distractions."

"Yes, sir," we both say together.

"Then get out there."

Anton and I jog out on the field and line up with the others, but as soon as we start to run through plays as a team, I can tell that everyone's mind is distracted by the thought that the school might close down. We make mistake after mistake. Even the seniors are upset—it would be strange to say that you graduated from a school that no longer exists.

"Again," Coach yells when we mess up a play. "We will stay here until you get this right. I have all night, gentlemen."

Coach moves me to defense for a few plays and tells me to be prepared to play not only fullback but safety too. The kid who usually plays this position, Joe Warner, sprained his ankle during last Friday's game. He tried to practice on it today but only made it worse. He's sitting on the bench now, with his cleat off and a bag of ice on his foot.

Coach heads over there to talk to him and puts Anton in charge.

I make my way to the defensive line. Anton calls a play, but the center hikes the ball too short. It hits the ground, and just as Anton reaches down to pick it up, our biggest defenseman, Junior Jones, charges through the offensive line like a bull on fire. I can't do anything to stop him. I can only watch as he flies into Anton, head down. There is a crack of helmets and Anton is knocked off his feet. He falls backward and hits the ground. Hard.

The rest of us have enough sense to block Coach's view. He doesn't need to see the mess we just made out of a simple play. Two players down. Head-on collision.

"Sorry, man, sorry," Junior says slowly as he stands up. He reaches down to help Anton up, but Anton is still out of it. He's sitting, but he's not ready to stand.

"You really hit him, Junior," someone says.

"What were you thinking?" I growl at Junior.

"I broke through the line. That's what I was supposed to do. Break through fast and hard."

"You just smashed into our quarterback," I say. "Our starting quarterback. The guy on our team who puts points on the board."

"It was an accident," he says, turning around and looking back at Coach who is still talking to Joe over on the bench. "I wasn't trying to crash into him. Don't say anything to Coach. He'll bench me."

I glare at Junior, but we both know I won't say anything. We can't afford to lose Junior at our game on Friday. I turn to Anton. "Are you okay?" I ask, helping him up.

Anton gives me a nod, but I can tell he's hurting.

"What's going on?" Coach bellows when he finally looks up and notices that we are at a standstill out on the field. We scramble to get back into position and start the play again.

This time, when the ball is hiked to Anton, he fumbles it.

Coach blows his whistle.

We run the play five times before we get it right. Anton keeps making mistakes. It isn't like him to play sloppy and miss his mark.

"You aren't focused! If you play like this on Friday night, this team is going to lose. What do you need to do to win?"

"Play focused. Play fast. Play efficient!" we all shout.

"Then start again. From the beginning. We run these plays until they're flawless. No mistakes."

Anton's face is pale, but he pushes through like always.

After an extra hour of practice, Coach finally tells us to go home. The blue sky above us has turned dark and gray. Storm clouds have moved in, and there is now a damp October chill in the air.

When we leave the locker room, Anton hands me the keys to his truck. At first I laugh, thinking he's joking. Anton has never let me drive his truck; he doesn't even let me eat or drink in it—not a sip of soda, not one chip. He worked overtime on a road construction crew over the last two summers to save up enough money to buy the truck from his neighbor. But when I look over I can tell Anton is serious.

"That bad?" I ask.

"Just drive," he says. "My head is killing me."

We climb in and I look over at him. I didn't think the hit was that bad. He seemed to be fine. I've taken my fair share of hits. You've just got to shake it off and push through— everybody on the team does. Usually Anton doesn't put on such a show about it, but I guess he's probably nervous about the big game.

As I pull out of the parking spot, I see Ciara heading to her car after soccer practice. I drive slowly past her and wave. She smiles and waves back.

"Two hands on the wheel," Anton says, smirking at me, then grimacing. "Do not crash this truck."

As I turn out of the school parking lot, the rain starts to fall. It is hard and fast and sounds like someone is tapping their knuckles against the roof.

Chapter 7

Two days later, on Friday, when Anton picks me up for school, I'm surprised that he isn't pumped up for the game. He was sluggish at practice the day before, but he told me he was just tired. I thought he'd be fine today. He has fought hard to play through every game since his first day on the team.

I turn up the radio to blast some music like we normally do, but he reaches over and turns it off. I look over at him annoyed.

"What's up with you?" I ask.

"I just . . . I can't get rid of this headache," he says.

"Still?" I say, surprised. When I've taken my bad hits I've always bounced back after a day or two. So has Anton. "Did you take some aspirin?"

"Yeah," he says. "It doesn't do a thing."

"You'll be fine once you get out on the field tonight," I say, sure he just needs to start the game to get back in shape. That is how it is for me. Once the clock on the scoreboard starts ticking backward and the adrenaline takes over, whatever is bothering me fades away completely. All my focus is on the game.

Anton nods his head at this and doesn't say anything the rest of the drive to school. Usually he's reciting all the stats on the players from the opposing team, but not today.

***

Since it's game day, there's a pep rally in the gym before classes start. The band is playing, the cheerleaders are bouncing around, but the students in the stands are all somber. Word has spread that our school might be closing.

I'm hoping Anton will make some kind of

big speech to get everyone in the gym riled up, but he doesn't. He acts just like he did in the truck this morning.

Instead of his normal pep talk, all he manages to get out is a halfhearted "Go Wolves!" before handing the microphone back to Coach. Everyone else seems taken aback too. He usually likes to talk and get the crowd pumped up. *Maybe*, I think, *he's taking this game more seriously because the school is on the line.*

"Come on," I say to him as Coach gives a short speech. "We need to get some good energy going."

"I can't yell right now," Anton says. "I can't even think."

I look around the gym. The students in the stands seem defeated. It's as if a decision for our school has already been made. As much as I hate public speaking, I don't want our pep rally to end like this. So when Coach is done, I ask for the microphone.

I look around at all the students. "This is our school!" I shout. "Warren High!"

The students start to perk up.

"This is our team! The Warren Wolves!"
The guys behind me all let out a howl. "And
we aren't going down without a fight! Stand up
if you love this school!"

Students begin to clap and then stand.
They begin to stomp. They begin to howl.

Chapter 8

At lunch Anton isn't sitting at our table. Someone tells me they saw him head out to his truck. I figure he just wants to be somewhere quiet for a while, but when I don't see him in Ms. Jenkins's science class, I get worried. Anton isn't the type of kid to skip class or miss a test. Even on game days, he's focused in the classroom. He's pushed me to get better grades and helped edit my papers since we became friends. He always reminds me that I can't play if I let my grades drop.

I set my books down, tell Ms. Jenkins I need to use the bathroom, and run out to the parking lot, where I find Anton sound asleep in the cab of his truck.

I knock on the window. He opens his eyes and looks at me like he has no idea where he is.

"We have a test!" I yell. "Science. Ms. Jenkins. Now."

Anton unlocks and opens the door.

I repeat what I just said because it doesn't seem like he heard me the first time.

Suddenly, he seems to get it. "I totally forgot," he says, scrambling to gather up his stuff.

We hurry back to class and enter the room just as Ms. Jenkins begins to hand out the test.

"You're late," she tells Anton. He doesn't say he's sorry. Ms. Jenkins gives him a quizzical look. Anton is Mr. Manners most of the time. The teachers love him at our school, but I can tell that Ms. Jenkins isn't loving him so much right now. She hands him a test and he slides into his desk.

For the first time in my life, I finish a test before Anton does. When I go to turn it in, I see him put his head down on his desk and close his eyes. Ms. Jenkins walks by, leans over him, and asks him if he's sick.

He shakes his head and sits back up. I can tell that Ms. Jenkins is concerned. She holds him after class, and when I ask Anton about it, he tells me that he told her that he was just worried about the game, that he hadn't slept the night before, but she didn't believe him and wanted him to see the nurse.

"There is no way I'm going down there," he says to me as we walk down the hall. "The nurse will call home, and my mom will get all worked up. I can't handle that. Not right now."

I nod at this as Anton stops at the drinking fountain and takes another aspirin.

"You'll be fine," I say, hoping that a pep talk is what Anton needs to get back in the zone. "You made it through practice yesterday, you can make it through this game. Remember when Byron Leftwich played with a cracked tibia? Brett Favre with a broken thumb? You don't have broken bones. A headache is nothing compared to that."

Anton takes another drink of water, looks at me and says, "Don't worry, I'm playing tonight. Playing to win."

Chapter 9

Before our game, Anton and I stand on a small hill just outside our locker room and look down at the football field below—at the bright lights, the green grass, the freshly painted white lines.

"This is it," Anton says. "This is everything."

He reaches in his jacket pocket and takes out a bottle of aspirin. He takes two pills and washes them down with a swig of an energy drink.

"Is your headache any better?" I ask.

"Yeah," he says, but I see his forehead

scrunch up. "I'll be fine."

"You always pull this team through," I say. "You're our ticket to a win."

Behind us a car door slams in the parking lot. I hear laughter and turn around and see Ciara Johnson and some of her soccer teammates pile out of an old minivan. She's wearing a white knit hat and her soccer warm ups. Her dark, curly hair is tied into two braids with silver ribbons at the end.

"Malcolm Busby," she yells and waves at me. I love the way she says my full name. Even the teachers have started calling me just Busby, but not Ciara Johnson. "You ready to win tonight?"

"Yeah," I say, smiling at her.

She waves and heads down the hill toward the stands. It kills me watching her go. I want to say something more. I want to stand with her on top of this hill and talk to her for more than two seconds, but I can't ever seem to get out more than three words when she's around.

Anton is watching me watch Ciara.

"Ask her out!" he says. "Text her. Call her.

Just stop staring at her. It's creepy."

I give him a soft punch on the shoulder.

"Let's just get going," I say, heading to the locker room. "You've got more important things to worry about than my love life. We've got to win this game."

Chapter 10

In the locker room, I'm already dressed before Anton even gets his locker open. He looks tired, and I want to shake him and wake him up. Just like at the pep rally, he's not fully himself. He's the guy who usually gets us all pumped up. We need him right now. We need him to get some good energy going in the room. We need him to snap out of this funk. But he's just putting on his gear—slowly, methodically.

"Is he sick?" Corbin Jensen asks, a little too hopeful. He's a sophomore and our second-string quarterback.

"No," I say. "He's fine."

"He didn't look fine the other day."

"He's good," I say. "Just focusing on the game."

Corbin looks disappointed by this, and I look at him and say, "You better hope he's all right. You better hope he can play. He's the only one who can make a pass on this team."

I fill up my water bottle and look back at Corbin. The kid isn't ready to play against a team like the Titans. He doesn't have the strength. He doesn't have the arm. But mostly, he doesn't have the same passion as Anton.

Coach Quimbley steps into the locker room, and we all take a knee. He waits for every one of us to look up at him.

"I'm not going to lie to you," Coach says. He takes off his baseball hat and runs his fingers through his hair. "The Titans are tough, and we're going to have to dig deep tonight to pull out a win. But I've watched you this season—I've watched each and every one of you play with grit and heart. And tonight, I know you are going to play to win not only for this team, but for this school. For this town."

We all nod somberly at this. If we don't win, we may never play together again.

Coach motions to Anton to take us out. We huddle up and put one hand in the middle of the circle. Anton puts his hand on top of ours and counts off: "One. Two. Three."

"Protect the pack!" We all yell at once.

As I put my helmet on, I see Coach pull Anton aside. I know Coach must have noticed that Anton's been off since Wednesday, and I hope Anton can pull himself together. We need him to play.

Chapter

11

Out on the field, our small cheer squad does their best to rile up the crowd. They cup their hands around their mouths, fling their heads back, and howl up at a sky.

I don't remember ever seeing so many fans or hearing so much noise, but I think everyone has the same thought I have—a year from now this field could be silent, the white lines faded, the grass overgrown.

Anton nods at number 46 of the Titans. The guy is huge. At least six foot four and close to three hundred pounds.

"Ellison Green," Anton says. "He's gotten

nineteen sacks this season alone."

"Then don't let him get you," I say with a smile, but when I look over at our bench, I know our team is in trouble. We don't have guys that size. To make the team look bigger than it really is, Coach Quimbley has suited up half a dozen freshmen, but we all know he'll never send them out. Piled up together on a scale, those freshmen probably wouldn't weigh as much as Ellison Green.

We head to our bench. Behind us are our fans. Ciara Johnson is in the front row— she's laughing and clapping along with some cheer. I wave to her, but she doesn't see me. I wish she did. I want her to yell out my name. *Malcolm Busby!* I feel like it would bring me some luck.

A few rows to the left, I see my mom sitting by herself. She waves to me. I wave back and wish my dad were in the stands too, but he couldn't make it home this weekend. His supervisor needed him to work overtime.

Anton doesn't even glance at the stands. He knows his parents aren't there. His mom can't watch, and his dad has taken a trucking job, so he's gone most of the time just like mine.

"Let's warm up your arm," I suggest to Anton who is just sitting on the bench. He needs to get his energy up. Usually by this point he's pumped up, moving up and down the bench talking to everyone.

We head to the sideline and throw the ball, but his throws are weak and off target.

"I feel like I'm walking through a swamp," he says shaking his head.

"Remember when you played the day after you had the stomach flu? You started off slow but then threw three touchdowns. You had a great game," I remind him.

"Yeah," Anton says. "That's right. I did."

"You can do this!" I say. "Push through!"

He throws the ball again, this time it has some speed, but it goes wide. A few more passes and he's getting closer to target. The referee blows his whistle. Three minutes to kickoff. I guess that will have to do.

Coach sends Anton and I out on the field

for the coin toss. Two huge players from the other team, one of them is number 46, meet us out on the field. It's as if their coach has sent them out to intimidate us.

"Heads," Green calls with a confident smile. I watch the silver dollar flicker through the air and land on the grass—heads up.

The Titans decide to receive the kick. We will defend.

Anton and I head back to our team and gather around Coach. He nods at the Titans' special teams as he unwraps a stick of cinnamon gum and shoves it in his mouth. Then he says to me, "Busby, if a tornado were about to touch down on the field, I do believe you'd find a way to take it down."

"Yes, sir," I say.

"Well, I got word that their tight end, number 23, is fast, so be ready. I'm sending you out there too. We can't let the Titans get a touchdown on their first drive. Find a way to stop him."

His breath is all cinnamon and red hot, but his words are calm and cool.

I head out onto the field, but when I see that Green is heading out there too, I realize that there may be more than one tornado I need to stop.

Chapter 12

We line up. Our kicker sets up and kicks the ball. It is a high, long kick.

We rush down the field.

Most of the time, my thoughts rush around in my brain like a swarm of mosquitoes, but out on the field everything slows down. Fortunately this game is no different—my thoughts are focused and clear.

As the ball descends, I know that 23 will make the catch. I see him take a few steps forward, his arms out front, and before the ball is even in his hands, I know he'll run straight up the middle. I see him plant his back leg and turn his shoulder.

I'm ready to strike.

Heart racing, legs pounding, I head straight for him. But Green cuts between us. I put my right shoulder out, and ram into his chest, but I just bounce off the giant number 46 on the front of his jersey and land on the ground, the breath knocked out of me. Number 23 leaps over me, but I manage to reach up and grab his left leg to bring him down. He falls hard.

A whistle blows and the crowd roars. I can tell 23 is hurting.

I reach down to help him up, but he doesn't take my hand. Instead, number 46 gets in my face. His eyes are the color of mud, and he smells like sour milk.

"Heard your team won't even exist next year—that the Wolves are dead."

I move closer to him. Our facemasks are just a few inches apart.

"You heard wrong," I say. "We aren't going anywhere."

"Yeah, right," he says with a laugh. "Your whole town isn't going anywhere. It's all washed up."

I push him in the chest, and a referee comes over to separate us. When we line up again, I stare him down. The Titans' center snaps the ball, Ellison Green goes left, and I go right. I tackle 23 as soon as he catches the ball. I hit him hard midstride and knock the ball out of his arms. One of our players pounces on it, and now it's ours.

Chapter 13

"**N**ice job," Coach says when I come off
the field. "You not only took down 23, but
rattled his confidence. He knows he's not
unstoppable anymore."

Coach sends me back out on the field,
this time, to play the position I know best—
fullback. I see the Titans' coach send Ellison
Green back out too. It looks like the two of
us will be going head-to-head this game, but
he's at least fifty pounds heavier than me and
four inches taller. I have no idea how to stop
the moving force of a guy like that. I glance at
Anton and know that I have to find a way to

protect him and keep the pocket open.

Our team huddles up, but Anton struggles to call the first play. As I look over at him I'm actually starting to get really angry with him. He's had every play in the book memorized since our first day of practice our freshman year. I don't understand why he can't just focus on this game rather than complaining about his stupid headache or worry about the school.

"A post route," I say to him looking back at Coach.

Anton nods at this. I take over. "We need to get on the scoreboard," I say, and then I look at our offensive lineman. "Whatever you do, don't let 46 through. Block hard, block low."

We line up and Green is staring at me again.

I don't look away. I watch to see which way his body is positioned, trying to figure out where he's going to go.

"Hut!"

Anton pulls back to throw. We buy him some time, but he's slow, unsteady. He gets pressured and throws the ball out-of-bounds.

"What was that?" I yell at him.

He just shakes his head

"Get it together," I say. "We need to get a first down."

I've never yelled at him out on the field. He's never one to make mistakes, but we need him to snap out of it and get his head in the game.

We line up again. Same play. I signal for two linemen to block 46 on the right. I can see his back foot turn that way. Anton steps back and throws, but it's weak and low. One of the Titans' players picks off the ball.

I turn and chase, but Ellison Green takes me down. And just like that, the Titans are ahead. They kick the extra point and it's 7–0.

Our crowd is quiet; I feel the disappointment in the air. We should've scored first. This is our field. This is our school.

Chapter 14

After Anton throws another interception that the Titans run back for a touchdown, we're down even further. They kick the extra point to make it 14–0.

Coach pulls Anton out and puts Corbin in. He's never pulled Anton before, and Anton slumps down on the bench, hanging his head.

"You've got to push through whatever fog you're in," I say when I'm back on the sideline. "We need you in this game."

Anton nods at this but doesn't look up. I want to shake him; he's only half here, but he knows how important this game is. We need to get points up on the board. We need to win.

"We run the ball," Coach says at the start of the second quarter. He's got at least three sticks of gum in his mouth, which isn't a good sign. His cinnamon breath hangs in the air, and it feels like it could burn you if you get too close. "Corbin is going to throw short, quick passes, and the receivers are going to run like they've never run before. You need to be strong out there. Poke some holes in their defense. Our main objective right now is to hold onto the ball and move it down the field."

We all nod at this and head back out. As we walk across the field, I warn Corbin about 46. Corbin can't weigh more than 145 pounds, and I know Green will crush him like an aluminum can if he gets the chance.

Corbin lines up and messes up the first play. He looks to pitch a lateral left, but he's supposed to go right, and when he can't find his man, he panics, steps back, and holds onto the ball too long.

Ellison Green rushes our line. I throw my body in front of him in an attempt to stop him from sacking Corbin. Green stumbles and falls on top of me. As we go crashing to the ground, I spin around to take one last look at Corbin before I'm pinned facedown beneath number 46.

Green pretends to struggle to get up, but what he's really doing is pressing down on my helmet so my face mask digs into the turf. I finally get out from under him and push him in the chest, knocking him on his butt.

A ref calls a penalty on me and we lose fifteen yards. I know Coach is probably really mad.

I don't even look over at the sideline. I just head over to the huddle and wipe the grass and dirt from my mask.

"What is Coach calling?" Corbin says to me. "What play is that."

I look over and see Anton standing next to Coach. At first, I think he's going to send Anton back in, but then I realize we don't have time.

"A screen pass," I say as I lock eyes with Anton and he nods. I know Anton called the play, which is a good sign. He's got his head back in the game. He knows we can't beat the Titans physically, but we can turn their strength against them with a little deception.

"We got this," I say to Corbin. "Just stay calm and cool. This play is fun."

"Fun?" Corbin mumbles.

"Lots of fun," I say with a smile.

Corbin takes the snap, and our linemen spring into action. I act like I'm going to step up to block Ellison Green, but instead I roll out into the flat. Green runs past me, and he and the defensive line head straight toward Corbin who is holding onto the ball. But when they get close, Corbin lofts a short pass over their heads. I catch it and run behind three of our blockers. They all go low and hard and make perfect blocks. I run down the sideline. It's just me and the Titans' safety. One on one. I can't outrun him, so at the last minute I bend my knees, lower my shoulder, and run right into his chest. He stumbles backward and falls. I stay on my feet and accelerate into the end zone.

Touchdown!

And the kick is good.

Titans 14. Wolves 7.

Our fans howl. They roar. And I hold up the ball for them all to see. I feel like we can win this—like we have a chance.

Chapter 15

Anton is smiling at me when I get back to the bench.

"You got us on the board," he says. He seems like he wants back in the game, but Corbin has earned some plays. Coach doesn't put Anton back in.

Right before halftime, Corbin stumbles and panics again. He tries to run with the ball, but Green knocks through our offensive line. When I go low to stop him, he leaps right over me and sacks Corbin. Bam! Corbin fumbles the ball and falls to the ground as the Titans pounce on it.

I look back over at Corbin. Ellison Green is on top of him. When he stands up, I see Green step on Corbin's hand and lean into his cleat with all his weight. Corbin cries out in pain, and Green puts his arms up like he's sorry. Like it was an accident. But I saw it all and I know better. I go after him, push him from behind, and another penalty gets called on me. Me! Nothing is called against him even though Corbin is writhing in pain on the field.

I argue with the referee. I point to Corbin's hand, but the ref threatens to kick me out of the game. Coach benches me until I calm down. With a minute left on the clock, the Titans march down the field and kick a field goal.

At the end of the half we are down 17–7.

Chapter 16

In the locker room during halftime, our team looks like we've been smashing into a brick wall. We are battered and bruised. Corbin is soaking his hand in a pail of ice. When he pulls it out, it's red and swollen. I can tell it's broken from my seat on the bench six feet away.

"Don't take me out," Corbin pleads. "I can't throw, but I feel like I could take someone down right now."

Coach puts his hand on Corbin's shoulder, "You need an X-ray."

"I'm not leaving this game."

"I'm not putting you back in," Coach says, and he starts to wrap Corbin's hand. I can see the pain in Corbin's face, and I want to take Ellison Green down and squash his nose.

When he's done with Corbin's hand, Coach looks up at all of us.

"You can't play angry or reckless out there. You have to play for the love of the game, for the love of this school. If you play for revenge, you'll play dumb, and we'll lose. Play smart. Play focused. Play strong."

As we put our helmets back on and get ready to take the field again, I see Coach talking to Anton, and I see Anton nodding his head.

"What did he say?" I ask Anton as we walk back on the field.

"He wants me to throw some long passes."

"You've got this," I say to him.

"I don't know," he says. "I don't trust my throwing tonight. I told Coach to keep calling trick plays. We need to throw the Titans off. Do things they don't expect. I need to warm my arm back up."

"You've got this," I say. "*We've* got this."

"We do." Anton nods, and we head back to the field.

Chapter 17

The Titans kick. Our returner runs out-of-bounds at the ten-yard line. We have a long way to go, but we are determined. Play after play, first down after first down, we push until we are in Titans territory.

At third and twenty, we are winded but still pushing. Anton pretends the ball is tucked under his arm, but he has quietly set the ball on the ground. He looks like he's going to run, but as the Titans' defense approaches, he shows his hands. No football. One of our lineman, Reece Larsen, has picked it up, tucked it under his arm, and started running down the field.

The Titans didn't see it coming. When they finally go after Reece, it's too late.

Touchdown!

The Titans cry foul, but it's a legal play. The ball touched the ground first. Green is mad. He's yelling about cheap tricks. Kicking at the turf. Spitting on the ground. The ref sends him to the bench.

Coach calls for a two-point conversion. The Titans form a wall, but we move as if we are one giant beast. Our receiver crosses over the line and Anton throws the ball in a spectacular arc that lands right in our receiver's hands.

Titans 17. Wolves 15.

We are back.

Chapter 18

At the start of the fourth quarter Coach calls me over.

Number 23 and Ellison Green are both heading out on the field.

"I'm going to keep sending you out there on defense," Coach says. "Keep your eyes on 23. Their QB is going to throw him the ball."

I can feel myself starting to drag, but I know that if Anton can push through, I can too.

The Titans line up and they don't look tired at all. They look like it's the start of the first half. The Titans QB throws a pass right to number 23, and I go after him, but he outmaneuvers me, catches the ball, and runs down the field for another touchdown.

Titans 23. Wolves 15.

I feel like I've let everyone down. I should've stopped him. I should've watched him more carefully. We were so close; now it feels so far away, but Anton has our bench pumped up.

"We can do this," he's yelling. "It isn't over. We can pull out the win. Dig. Dig deep!"

Anton's energy is contagious. When the Titans try to go for the conversion, we stop them in their tracks. During our possession Anton throws a nice twenty-yard pass, but the Titans' defense starts going after our receivers. If we keep trying to throw, there's a chance the ball will get intercepted again, so now we have to try running the ball. We make it down to the thirty-yard line and kick a field goal.

We are still behind as the Titans take possession of the ball. They run it down the field and work to burn time off the clock, but I decide to channel Ellison Green. At third and ten at the fifty-yard line, I power into their offensive line, find a hole, and sack their quarterback. He fumbles the ball, and I pounce on it and don't let go.

Coach calls a timeout.

"You still have legs?" He asks me. I'm tired. I'm sore. I've been playing both ways all game, but I look at him and nod my head. "Yes."

"Then you are going back in." He then looks at Anton. "You are going to throw that ball with all you've got. I want all the receivers down in the end zone. Anton is going to throw, and one of you is going to catch it. That is our play. Throw and catch."

Anton looks energized and confident as we head out.

"You're back," I say.

"I am," he says. "Just buy me a little time."

The center makes a sloppy snap to Anton, but he catches it with one hand. It takes him a second to get his balance back. I get ready to block. Anton needs some time.

Our lineman smash with all their might into the Titans' defense as three receivers run down the field. I'm supposed to run too, but I see that Green has broken through. He's going to take Anton down. Somebody has to stop him. I have to stop him. So I put my shoulder down and block him with everything I've got. We push against each other. I hold him in place for a few seconds. Just as Anton launches the ball, Ellison Green gets loose and nails Anton with a late hit.

Anton didn't see Green coming. He flies backward and the back of his head crashes against the ground. No one else seems to see Anton's fall; everyone else is watching the ball and then the catch. Everyone in the stands is jumping up and down. Our team is in the end zone celebrating. We've scored with two seconds left on the clock. We've won.

I run over to Anton. He doesn't move. He doesn't respond, and when he finally opens his eyes, he looks like he doesn't know where he is. But he reaches for me, and I help him sit up.

"You okay?" I ask him.

"Did we win?"

I laugh at this and say, "Yeah, man. We won. We're going on to the playoffs."

"We won?" He asks again as I help him stand up. He's wobbly and leans on me.

"Yeah," I say. I feel like I'm talking to a little kid. Our team runs down the field and sweeps us up. Then we are all mobbed by the fans from the student section rushing onto the field. Suddenly Ciara is standing in front of me. Her arms loop around my neck, and she's hugging me and saying, "Nice job, Malcolm Busby. Nice game!"

Chapter
19

In the locker room Anton looks pale, but he's smiling.

"How are you feeling?" I ask.

"Like I got run over by a truck."

He lies down on the bench, but the other guys from our team pull him back up. They make him celebrate. They jostle him around. He's usually the one leading the celebration party in the locker room, but now he's flopping around like a rag doll, trying to break loose so he can sit back down.

"Playoffs! Playoffs!" the team starts to chant.

"The pack is back!" someone else yells.

Anton sits back down on the bench. He drinks from his water bottle.

"You're acting like we lost!" Junior scowls at him.

"Just worn out," Anton says. "Celebrating inside."

He puts a fist against his heart.

Junior laughs.

We keep celebrating and Coach doesn't even try to give a speech; he just writes across the white board in bright red letters: playoffs. be ready. next friday night. this is our year. Anton tries to smile and howl with the rest of us, but I can see he's in pain. I find him some more aspirin and get him some water. I take a couple of pills too—my shoulder is killing me.

The shower makes me feel a little bit better, but when I get out, I find Anton still in his uniform, sitting on the bench. Most of our team is already changed and heading out to Pizza Barn.

"You want me to bring you home?" I ask Anton.

"Nah," he says. "Free pizza tonight."

Herb Cozzette, the owner of Pizza Barn, promised to feed our team and fans for free if we made it into the playoffs this year.

"Hurry up, then," I say to Anton.

By the time he's finally showered and dressed, we are the last ones out of the locker room, and Coach is waiting outside to lock up.

"Boys," he says to us. "You made me proud tonight. You worked hard. You didn't give up." Then he looks at Anton. "How are you feeling? I've been told you took a hit right at the end. Nothing we can do about it now, but I want to make sure you are okay."

"I'll be good in the morning," Anton says, forcing a smile. "No big deal."

"You rest up. Take it easy this weekend."

Anton nods at this.

When we get to his truck, he hands me his keys again and crawls into the passenger side. As he closes his eyes he mumbles, "Just when the headache was finally gone, I get smacked in the head again. Ellison Green is lucky he graduates this year. He'd get taken out by our team if we ever played him again."

I feel bad for not stopping Green, and I can tell this second hit was a hard one. Anton's face is a dull gray color. His words are slightly slurred. I'm a little worried about him.

Chapter 20

We are the last ones to arrive. There's a bonfire burning in the parking lot, and music blaring from the speakers of someone's car. It has been years since the Wolves have made it to the playoffs, but we've finally done it again.

I hear people talking about us making it to state, and I know it's a long shot, but I feel like anything is possible after tonight's game. We pulled out a win against one of the best Northern teams in the state. We beat the Titans. And I hope Ellison Green is crying into his pillow somewhere.

Herb is standing up on a picnic table. A

huge grin on his face. "Busby, number 50, and Anton, number 12, get on up here! Where have you been? We've been waiting for you to arrive."

Anton and I look at each other, but we don't say anything as we head over to the table. Anton is a little wobbly getting up. I try to hide my concern from everybody else, but Herb notices.

"My pizza will cure him in no time," Herb whispers to us. "He needs to get his strength back."

When we are both on top of the table, Herb's wife hands him two pizzas with our numbers written out in pepperoni.

"I'm proud of these kids," Herb says, and the crowd quiets down. "I'm proud of this team," and then he looks at Anton and everyone waits for him to say something, but he just stands there completely silent for a minute.

"Thank you," he finally says, shaking Herb's hand. "Thank you everyone for coming out to tonight's game." Then he nods at me.

"Busby! Busby! Busby!" the crowd chants.

For the second time today, I watch Anton leave a crowd primed for a speech. He steps down from the table and hands his pizza to Junior before disappearing into the crowd. He leaves me just standing there.

"Uhh, thank you for coming out and supporting us." My voice is quiet and unsure. I don't think I like being the spokesperson for the team. Anton definitely does a better job.

"Louder," someone yells.

So I look at that crowd, I look at my teammates and think *what would Anton do?* I immediately know the answer. I tilt my head back and yell at the top of my lungs: "The Wolves live on!"

The crowd lets out a howl and I howl too. I hope the town hears our voices rise up in the night air. The Warren Wolves aren't going to be stopped. We are still strong.

Feeling like I've done my job, I start to get down, but Coach climbs up on the table and makes me stay. "I have the game ball right here." The crowd claps. "And tonight's game ball goes to Busby. He played defense and offense. He was out on the field leading this team. He got us our first touchdown. And got us fired up! So this is for you."

He hands me the ball and I hold it up.

"Busby! Busby!" the crowd chants again. And I want to keep winning. I want to keep playing. I want our team to make it all the way to state.

Chapter

21

Ciara Johnson comes up to me right as I'm biting into a slice of pizza. There is cheese and grease on my chin.

"You need to come and get Anton," she says. "He's puking in the parking lot."

I quickly set down the pizza and follow her through the crowd to the back of the parking lot.

Anton is leaning up against his truck and wiping his face.

"Man, you don't look good," I tell him.

Anton doesn't even look up at me.

"What is up with him?" Ciara asks.

"He got hit pretty hard at the end of the game." Anton looks weak and shaky. I've never seen him this sick before, even when he had the flu last year. His pale face scares me.

"I wonder if he got a concussion," she says, backing away as Anton heaves again. "I got one in a soccer game two years ago, and it messed me up. I don't remember the hit or the end of the game, but I do remember puking like this."

"I'm fine," Anton barely whispers.

"You're not fine," I say as I dig in his truck for a water bottle and hand it to him. He takes a swig.

"I should take you home," I go on, trying not to sound too frantic. "Your mom should take you to a doctor or something."

He shakes his head, "My mom will get all freaked out and drag me into an ER, and we don't have money for that. I'll be fine. I just need to shut my eyes. I just need some sleep."

"We need to call someone," I insist. "You're not okay, dude."

"No," he says as he opens the door of his truck, crawls in, and lies down.

"Seriously," Ciara says. "You have to call his parents."

"I'll be fine," Anton says. "It just takes a few days."

"Concussions can be really bad," Ciara responds. She turns to me. "He needs someone to look at him."

She peers in the truck and then looks back at me. "Let's take him to Dr. Wilson," she says. "He lives next door to me. He doesn't charge for advice. He's been helping a lot of people out since he moved back a year ago."

I'm immediately relieved that Ciara has come up with a solution, but then I look down at my phone. "It's almost ten o'clock," I say.

"He'll still be up. I see his lights on until midnight most nights."

I glance over at Anton. He doesn't look good.

"Hey." I try to get his attention. He opens one eye and looks at me, annoyed. "We need to get you checked out."

Ciara walks around the front of the truck and gets in the driver's side and slides over to the middle.

"This isn't necessary," Anton says, sitting up and shifting over to give her room.

"You smacked your brain," Ciara says. "It's kind of an important organ."

"Fine," Anton grunts. It seems like he's too tired to argue anymore.

I get into the driver's seat.

"Thanks," I say to Ciara who is sitting next to me.

"No worries." She smiles at me. "Dr. Wilson is a great guy. I know he'll help."

As I drive, we sit in silence. I want to say something to Ciara—now would be my chance. But I can't stop thinking about how pale Anton's face looks and how unsteady he's been since his last hit.

We turn onto Main Street. There are a lot of empty buildings now. Half the businesses have closed. The bars are the only places that seem to turn a profit in this town. Families are leaving faster than they are coming in.

"Do your parents plan on leaving Warren?" I finally manage to get out as we drive by some homes for sale, still peering over at Anton every minute or two.

"They talk about it," she says. "But my dad is getting by doing work on cars. He wants to open up his own shop."

"That's great," I say, trying not to sound jealous. I wish my dad could've found some work in town.

"Yeah. But I'm hoping to get out of here. Go someplace far away after graduation. What about you?" Ciara turns to ask me. "What are you going to do when you graduate?"

I shrug my shoulders. "I'm just focused on our next game and trying to figure out how keep Warren High open so we can all walk across that stage together next spring. I don't want to graduate from some other school with a bunch of kids I don't know."

"It seem so wrong to split us up," Ciara says. "It won't feel right if I don't get to see you next year."

I look over at her and then back at the road. For a second I stop thinking about Anton completely. "Yeah," I say. "We can't let that happen."

Anton sits up and looks over at us, "Just date already."

I blush and look over at Ciara. She laughs. I don't know if the laughter is good or bad. All I know is that when I get Anton taken care of, I'm going to ask Ciara out on a real date.

Chapter

22

We park outside of the biggest house on Maple Street. It has a huge white porch that seems to wrap around to the back and red brick siding. Next door is a small, blue house with a rope swing hanging from an oak tree.

"That little house is mine." Ciara nods at it. "Six of us live in there, and Dr. Wilson lives all alone in the one next door."

"You ever ask him if he wants to trade?"

She nods and laughs at this.

I put the car in park then turn to Anton. "Let's get that big noggin of yours checked out." I'm feeling much better now that we've made a decision about what to do.

"This is dumb," Anton says. "I told you, I'm fine. I just need some sleep. And how do you know he won't charge me?"

"He won't," Ciara says. "Trust me. He does this for people all the time. It's what he does."

Anton doesn't move.

I look at him and say, "Get out. Or I'm dragging you out. We need you better before our next game."

Anton looks down at his hands and then finally slides out of the truck. This knock to the head has made him even more dramatic than when he was complaining about the headache after Junior sacked him at practice.

Ciara rings the doorbell and Anton and I stand behind her. An older man with silver hair opens the door. He's dressed in khaki pants, a dress shirt, and a blue blazer. He looks overdressed for a Friday night in this town.

"Ciara!" He sounds surprised. "Everything okay?"

"Dr. Wilson," she says, nodding to us. "Can you look at my friend? I think he might have a concussion, and we're not sure what to do."

"Of course." He looks over at Anton. "Come on in."

We follow him into a large entry way. There is a duffel bag and a suitcase sitting near the door.

"I'm sorry," Ciara says. "I forgot you're leaving tonight."

"I've got time." Dr. Wilson dismisses the apology. "My flight doesn't leave for a while."

"Where are you going?" I ask.

"Haiti," he says. "I'm heading down there to volunteer in a small medical clinic for a few weeks."

We walk through a living room and into a study that is set up like a doctor's office. There is an exam table in the middle of the room. Behind it are shelves filled with medical books and framed degrees.

"How did you hit your head?" Dr. Wilson asks Anton as we help him onto the exam table.

Anton looks at me, and I realize he doesn't even remember.

"A huge guy plowed into him at the end of

our game," I say. "He knocked Anton off his feet, and Anton hit the ground with the back of his helmet."

"Hmm," Dr. Wilson sighs. "What position do you play?"

"Quarterback," Anton says, shifting uncomfortably on the table.

Dr. Wilson nods at this. "I played for the Warren Wolves too. But that was many moons ago." He gives a crackly howl.

"What position did *you* play?" I ask.

"Wide receiver." He beams with pride. "Took some big hits myself, but luckily nothing major."

Dr. Wilson starts examining Anton. He looks at the back of Anton's head.

"And you don't remember this?" he asks Anton.

"I kind of do," Anton responds hesitantly.

"How long was he out?" Dr. Wilson asks me.

"Maybe ten or fifteen seconds?" I say.

He shines a flashlight into each of Anton's eyes and shakes his head.

"Your pupils are dilated," he says.

He opens a cabinet on the other side of the room and takes out a stethoscope and listens to Anton's heart and then checks his blood pressure, all while asking Anton a series of questions. *Have you had headaches? Have you felt tired? Are you sensitive to light?*

Anton answers yes to all of them.

"Well," Dr. Wilson finally says, "I can't confirm how bad it is without doing further tests with more equipment, but you definitely have a concussion."

Chapter 23

I start to speak, but before I can get a full word out Anton cuts in.

"We should go," Anton says quickly. "And really, I'm feeling better. It's nothing serious."

Anton clearly wants to bolt, but I have his keys and I want to hear what Dr. Wilson has to say. I feel even guiltier than when I first let Anton get hit.

"Let me make you some ginger tea," Dr. Wilson says. "It will help with the nausea."

He heads to the kitchen.

"Let's go," Anton says.

"Don't be rude," Ciara says. "Drink

some tea. It's the least you can do."

We follow Dr. Wilson into the kitchen and sit down at a round oak table.

Dr. Wilson busies himself making tea. He opens a package of cookies and passes them around. I take a few, but Anton shakes his head when I offer him one.

Dr. Wilson hands Anton a steaming mug.

"I don't feel sick anymore," Anton insists, looking at the tea as if Dr. Wilson has put poison in it.

Dr. Wilson sits in a chair next to Anton. His face is soft but serious.

"For the time being, you need to rest that brain of yours. No electronics, no screens. No reading. And no football."

"For how long?" we both say at the same time.

"At least five days. And if you have any sign of a lingering headache, you cannot step on that field. A second impact can cause cerebral edema and herniation. It can lead to permanent brain damage or death."

My heart feels like it has stopped. I look at

Anton and then at Dr. Wilson and interrupt, "This was his second hit to the head. He got hit two days ago and I made him play tonight."

"You didn't make me play," Anton snaps at me. "I played because I wanted to play."

Dr. Wilson frowns at this. "Did you have a headache after the first hit?"

"No," Anton lies. I look at Dr. Wilson and want to tell him that, *yes*, Anton had a headache—he was in a fog until halfway through our game.

"Tell me about the first hit."

"It wasn't a big deal," Anton says. "I don't know what Busby is even talking about. I just need to get home and get some sleep. I'll be better in the morning."

Dr. Wilson looks at me.

"Did you see the hit?"

"He wasn't even there," Anton interrupts. "He doesn't know what he's talking about."

I sit quietly in my chair, but I was there. I do know. I saw how much pain he was in before he even took the field tonight. Was that hit a concussion too? Did I just let him get his second concussion in three days?

Anton gets up and turns to me. "Give me my keys." He practically growls at me.

"Multiple head injuries need to be taken seriously," Dr. Wilson says. "They can be deadly."

He writes something down on a notepad and gives it to Anton.

"This is a note for your coach. You need to give this to him. And here is my card. I want your parents to call me. Tonight."

"I'm fine," Anton says shoving the piece of paper and card into his pocket. He turns to me and holds opens his hand, waiting for me to hand over his keys, but I don't budge.

"I'll drive you home," I say.

"Then let's go."

I know he's upset, but he's being a real jerk. This doctor has just taken care of him and saved him a trip to the ER. Maybe Anton isn't taking this seriously, but *I am*.

"One more thing," Dr. Wilson says. He scribbles down something else on a pad of paper and hands it to Anton. "Dr. Lydia

Anderson is a specialist down in the city. She's someone I want you to see if your headache worsens, if your vision becomes blurry, or if you have trouble concentrating."

He hands the second piece of paper to Anton, and Anton shoves it into the same pocket.

"My head doesn't even hurt anymore," he says. "I'm feeling good."

"Why don't you give me your parent's number?" Dr. Wilson says. "I can give them a call right now." But Anton just heads out of the kitchen, and I can hear him open the front door.

"Thank you," I say to Dr. Wilson. "I'll make sure he gets home okay." And then I turn to Ciara and say, "Thanks for everything. I'm sorry he's acting like this."

"I hope he really does feel better," Ciara says. "I hope he's going to be okay."

I hope so too.

Dr. Wilson walks me to the door. "That irritability you see is a symptom of a concussion. You need to make sure his parents call me. And you need to keep an eye him. He shouldn't be going to football practice, and he *definitely* should not be playing in any games. He should be in a dark room letting his brain recover until the symptoms are gone. If I didn't have to catch this flight, I'd drive out to his house and talk to his parents tonight, but I don't think I have enough time."

"I'll take care of him," I say.

Just then a car pulls up.

"My driver is here," Dr. Wilson says. "Please have Anton's parents call me. My flight leaves at midnight. I'll be able to talk while I'm in the airport, but I don't think I'll have any reception once I'm in Haiti. Take care of your friend. I'll check on him when I get back."

Ciara and I wave to him as he we head down the porch stairs.

Chapter 24

Anton is in the driver's seat when I get to the truck. I have to argue with him for five minutes before he agrees to let me drive him home.

"You can't say anything to my parents," he says. "My mom will get all crazy and we don't have any money for an ER visit right now. They have no savings left. I'll be fine. It isn't like I have broken arm or leg."

"You've broken your head," I say putting the truck in drive. I see Ciara walk to her house next door. She doesn't turn around before she disappears inside.

"My head isn't broken," Anton says. "I'm walking. I'm talking. There's no skull fracture. I'm fine."

"You aren't fine!" I think back to earlier in the night when I was trying to convince him that he was okay. When I made him play and get hit like this.

"I just need some sleep. I'll take it easy this weekend, and I'll be good as new on Monday."

I take a right and drive past our high school. I think of every brick being laid by hand. Brick by brick. Built by people in this town.

"You need to at least talk to coach," I say. "There's no way you should play in next week's game."

"I'm going to be fine," he says.

I pull into Anton's driveway, and I can see his mom sitting on the couch watching TV in their living room.

"Please don't say anything to her," Anton says. "You know how much she didn't want me to play football in the first place. This will just make her worry over nothing."

"It isn't nothing," I say, but even as I'm climbing out of the truck I'm not sure I have the heart to tell Anton's mom.

I grab my bag from the back of his truck and throw him his keys. He raises up his right hand to grab them, but misses. They clatter against the cement driveway.

I look at him.

"You need to tell coach."

He picks up the keys and turns to his house. I watch him go inside. I want to follow him in and talk to his mom, but I don't want to upset her—and I know Anton would never forgive me if I did.

Chapter 25

My mom is still up when I get home. She's in the kitchen making banana bread. She doesn't sleep well when my dad isn't around.

"You played great tonight," she says, giving me a hug. She smells like vanilla and brown sugar. "I'm so proud of you. I texted your dad the score."

The buzzer on the stove goes off and she pulls out two pans of bread.

I don't realize how hungry I am until the smell hits me. She carefully removes the bread from the pan and sets it on a plate as I grab the butter.

"Were you at Pizza Barn this whole time?"

"I didn't stay that long. Anton wasn't feeling great," I say quickly.

My mom cuts us each a slice of bread, and I spread a thick slab of butter on my piece. It melts and soaks into the bread.

"Careful," she says before I take a bite. "It's still really hot."

The bread tastes so good. I quickly devour it then cut myself another slice right away.

"It looked like Anton got taken down pretty hard by that big guy at the end of the game," she says. "Is he all right?"

I want to tell her about Dr. Wilson and Anton's concussions, but I know if I do, she'll call Anton's mom. I take another bite of bread and just nod at her.

"He's fine," I mumble. I'll see how he is in the morning. *Maybe Anton's right*, I think. *Maybe I'm making a big deal out of nothing.* But a louder voice in my head is telling me that Anton isn't all right. I'm just too much of a coward to tell anyone. I have to have Anton's back in this. I let him down on the field and I can't let that happen again.

"I got a call from your dad," my mom says. I had been so in my own head I had forgotten she was there. "He'll be here for your playoff game. He's sorry he missed tonight. He wants you to call him in the morning."

"How did he get off work?" I ask. "I thought they needed him to work all weekend."

"He found someone to fill in for him. He's driving back Thursday night," she answers. "He'll be here sometime Friday morning."

I worry about my dad driving all that way with little sleep, and I know my mom is worried about it too. I can tell by her face. There is a deep crease between her eyes.

"The bread is great," I say to make her think about something else. Something other than my dad driving through the night without sleeping.

"I could tell," she laughs and points to the empty plate.

I give her a hug, tell her goodnight, and walk down the hallway to my room. I wish my dad was home like he used to be. He was the one that first taught Anton and me how to play football, and he's basically like a second father to Anton. He would know what to do.

Chapter 26

Mondays are film day for the football team, so we head to the science lab after school. This classroom creeps me out—there are glass jars filled with parts of different animals floating in liquid and a skeleton wearing a knit hat with the wolf mascot on it.

"I feel like he's watching me," I say to Anton as he sits down on the stool next to me.

"Who?"

"The skeleton," I say.

"It doesn't have eyes." He sighs, putting his head down on his arms. "And Busby," he turns his head and looks at me, "stop bouncing your leg up and down like that or you are going to end up in one of those pickle jars."

I'm not good at sitting still. Waiting. Sometimes I don't even realize I'm bouncing my legs or tapping my fingers against a desk until someone tells me to cut it out. I look over at Anton. I don't know what to do about him. He's still not himself.

"Do you still have a headache?" I ask.

"I'm just really tired," he responds, sitting up. "It's Monday. I'm always tired on Mondays."

"Do you feel sick?"

"Seriously," Anton says looking at me. "When did you become my mom?"

I'm caught off guard. I've always looked out for Anton just like he's looked out for me. I'm about to reply when Coach walks in.

"Gentlemen," Coach Quimbley says, walking over to the projector screen at the front of the room.

"Good game Friday night!" We start to clap, but he holds up his hands. We all get quiet. Coach doesn't stand for any chatter on film day. "We won. Now we move on. We've got another team to beat. These guys have twelve talented seniors returning this year and a fast and powerful defense."

He looks at all of us sitting in the room and then his eyes stop on Anton.

"How are you feeling, Anton?"

"Great," Anton says forcing a smile. "Ready to get to work." But he doesn't look great to me.

"Good," Coach says. "The only way we'll win our next game is by passing the ball. Laterals. Long passes. Short passes. Sneak passes. The Hornets have a huge defensive line, so it's going to be tough to run the ball. We have to find their holes and figure out how to get our receivers through."

Coach picks up the remote, and we watch Hornet film. They're big and fast, and they know how to block, but they don't look as strong as the Titans. They don't have an Ellison Green or a number 23. I feel like we can beat them. I feel like we can take them down.

"What are their stats?" I whisper to Anton. His head is down on his arms again.

"I don't know," he mumbles. It isn't like him not to know the stats of at least the starting lineup. He usually has all that, plus all of the good backups, memorized by Monday.

"Anton," Coach snaps. "If you can't keep your head up to watch film, then how are you going to keep it up in the game?"

Anton sits up, but when he looks at the screen, I see him squint against the bright light of the film.

Chapter 27

After film, we have practice. Coach has warned us that we have to build up our strength. He's going to run us hard, and we're going to scrimmage on the field.

"You need to sit this one out," I say to Anton when he starts to pull on his gear.

"I'm fine." He glares at me.

"You need to talk to Coach and let him know you're not feeling so great. Tell him you are still getting over the flu or a cold or something."

"Seriously," Anton says, standing up and getting in my face. "I can take care of myself.

I need to get out there and throw the ball. How can we scrimmage if I'm not there? The team needs a quarterback. Corbin is still out. Who else can throw the ball? We all need to get ready for Friday's game. So don't worry about me, worry about winning."

I look at him and shake my head.

"Come on, just tell Coach you're sick. I'll throw the ball out there, and we can work on your arm when I get home."

"So you can do everything now? Be the star of the team? Is that what you want? To play quarterback? To take my place?"

I stare at him. I don't know this guy standing in front of me.

"You can't afford to get hit or take a fall," I say. "This isn't about me or the team. It's about that dumb brain of yours. Dr. Wilson said no practice or football until your headaches go away. Another hit could totally mess you up. It could kill you."

Anton puts on his cleats.

"You aren't going out there," I say. "It's just practice. Go home."

He ties his left shoe.

"Tell Coach you are sick, or I'll tell Coach what Dr. Wilson said."

Anton looks at me. He's mad now.

"Talk to him," I say again. I wish Dr. Wilson were still in town. I wish he would've called Anton's parents. I don't want to be the one to say anything. I know I'd be annoyed and angry if it were the other way around—if Anton was telling me I shouldn't practice. If he was bossing me around, telling me what I could and could not do. But I can't help but be scared that the next hit could take him out for good.

Anton kicks off his cleats and heads to Coach's office in his bare feet. I hear him knock and then see him disappear inside. And I want Coach to see what I see—Anton isn't right.

Chapter 28

I realize after practice that I have no ride home since Anton left like I told him to. I look around the locker room, but most of the other guys are already gone.

I head out to the parking lot, hoping that, if all else fails, I can get a ride with one of the freshmen who haven't been picked up yet. But as I open the door, I see a group of soccer girls clumped together chatting.

"Ciara," I call out when I see her curls bobbing up and down in the group. She's got her soccer cleats in her hands and looks like she's had a tough practice too.

"Malcolm Busby," she says coming over to talk to me. "How is Anton doing?"

"He tried to go to practice today."

"What?" She sounds serious. "Is he nuts?"

"I think he might be," I say. "He really isn't acting like the guy I know. He isn't thinking straight."

"You stopped him, right?"

"Yeah," I say. "But his parents and Coach still don't know he has a concussion. He won't let me tell them. He says he's fine, but I've seen him. He's not okay."

"You have to tell someone," Ciara says. "He could get hurt if he takes another hit. He's your best friend."

"I know. But . . ." I pause. "I don't think he'd ever forgive me if I say something, especially if he has to sit out for a playoff game." I'm a coward and I know it. I can't bring myself to tell somebody about Anton.

Ciara reaches up and hugs me. "I know it must suck. I don't mean to add more pressure to you. I'm sorry," she says.

When she lets go of me she's still standing

close. "Call me tonight. Let me know how things are going." I watch her walk away, almost forgetting why I came out to the parking lot in the first place. It isn't until she's almost to her car that I remember.

"Wait, Ciara," I call after her. "Can I get a ride home?"

She nods at this. Instead of going straight home, we stop at Pizza Barn and share a pizza. When she drops me off, I feel like we've been on a date, though I never really asked her out or anything. But I know it's a date when she leans over and kisses me before I get out of her car.

"Bye, Malcolm Busby," she says.

I stand at the end of my driveway as I watch her drive away, wondering what I should do next. I wish Anton wasn't so annoyed at me, because I'd call him. But I don't. I just go inside and try to do my homework. Then I call Ciara.

When I hear her voice, I just start talking. I don't have to think about what to say next. She's funny and smart, and we laugh. We make a plan to hang out after school on Thursday. I ask her this time.

Chapter

29

On Tuesday, Anton has made an excuse not to drive me to school. The two of us have driven together every day since the day he got his truck, and before that we rode the same bus. My mom has to drive me, and I feel like I'm back in first grade. Anton continues to ignore me—dodging me in the hallway and avoiding our lockers.

I finally see Anton in science class. I sit right behind him, but he barely talks to me. When we get our tests back, I see that Anton has failed. The kid has never failed a test in his life. There is red all over the page and at the top written in all caps the words: SEE ME.

After class, I see Ms. Jenkins talk to him. She knows something is wrong, but he won't tell her what it is. I watch him shake his head. When he comes out of the room, I want to say something to him, but I can tell he's upset he failed the test, and I know saying anything will just set him off. I don't know when to confront him, but I know now isn't a good time. I think about it all day, but Anton manages to continue to ignore me. For a guy who is supposed to be my best friend, he's really good at pretending he doesn't hear me call to him in the hallway.

***

"Anton!" I finally catch up with him after school as we head down to the locker room.

"How are you doing?"

"Big game Friday night," he says. "We're going to win it. I can feel it."

"So you're good?" I ask.

"Fine," he says. He doesn't look at me. He just heads straight into the locker room.

"Seriously," I say, grabbing his shoulder.

"Are you still having headaches?"

He turns and looks at me.

"No," he says. "If I were seriously injured, I wouldn't be at school. I wouldn't be here. But I'm walking and talking and going to practice today. Now drop it. There isn't anything wrong with me."

I believe him for a moment.

But when we are in the locker room, I see him taking more aspirin. He winces as he puts his shoulder pads over his head. I look around at the rest of the team. Most of us are banged up: the guys on our defensive line have bruises all up and down their arms; Corbin's hand is wrapped in a big cast; my right shoulder aches. But that doesn't stop the rest of us from going out there. Except I've realized, another hit to my shoulder won't kill me. Another hit to Anton's head just might put him in the hospital or worse.

Chapter
30

Instead of getting dressed, I go to Coach's office.

"Busby," he looks up from his playbook. "What do you need?"

"I need to talk," I say, sounding much more confident than I feel.

"Sit down," he points to the chair on the other side of his desk. I take a seat and my leg starts bouncing up and down nervously. I don't know if Anton will see it that way, but I'm doing the right thing. Coach needs to know, so I tell him about Anton's hit in practice and the hit at the end of the game and everything I can remember that Dr. Wilson said.

Coach takes out a pack of gum from the drawer of his desk and offers me a piece.

"Thanks," I say as I remove the foil and shove the stick of gum in my mouth.

"It's good you're telling me this," Coach says leaning back in his chair. I fold the gum wrapper over and over again until it is a tight, tiny square in my hand. "But you should've told me the first time Anton got a hit."

"We would've lost without him," I say.

Coach nods at this and then leans across his desk.

"Look at me," he says. Reluctantly, I meet his eyes. "I want to win a football game more than anyone, but my players come first. They always come first. On this team we take care of one another. We protect one another. We keep each other strong."

I nod at this.

"But we don't have another quarterback," I say.

"Maybe one of those freshmen has an arm we haven't yet seen." Coach shrugs, standing up. "There's always a player who surprises me, who steps up when we need him most. Thank you for stepping up. Thank you for putting your teammate first."

I watch Coach turn to the door. I feel guilty. I didn't put Anton first. I talked him into playing even when I knew he was hurt.

"Busby," he says, "I want you to be here when I talk to Anton. It will be better that way. He needs to know that you have his back not only out on the field but here—in this school, in life."

"He's asked me not to say anything to you. He's going to be mad."

"We'll talk to him," Coach says. "Together."

I nod my head at this.

Coach steps out of his office and I hear him call Anton's name.

I stare straight ahead at the wall behind Coach's desk. There are a dozen trophies on a shelf and a framed picture of our team taken early in September. I'm standing in front of Anton. He's just behind me in the back row. I don't look away from the picture until I hear Anton's footsteps just outside the office.

"Take a seat," Coach says when Anton comes to the door.

"I'm fine," Anton bursts out, not moving an inch past the doorframe, as if coming in would mean admitting defeat. "I don't know what Busby told you, but I'm all right. I took a hit, but I got back up; I had a little headache, but I'm totally fine now. I'm good. I saw a doctor and everything!"

Coach nods at the chair next to me.

"Take a seat."

Anton hesitates, but he knows not to question Coach. He walks past me, but he won't look at me. He sits in the chair, hands folded on his lap, looking straight ahead.

"You have a concussion," Coach says. "Possibly the second one in a week."

Anton looks down at his hands.

"I can't let you play," Coach says. "The risks are too great. Your health comes before anything else."

Anton nods at this, but he still won't look at me.

"I'm sorry," I say to Anton. "But your

headache has been really bad. You've seemed tired *all the time*. You aren't yourself. If we lose Friday's game, if our school closes down, we will all be okay. But you," the words catch in my throat, "if you take another hit, you might never recover."

Coach looks at me and then at Anton.

"Busby is absolutely right. You need to take care of that brain of yours. You need to protect it."

Coach then tells Anton that he's going to speak to his parents and that Anton can't practice or play until he gets a note from a doctor that says it's safe for him to take the field again.

Anton and I head out of Coach's office and back to the locker room in total silence. When we get to our lockers I'm about to say something when Anton sits down on the bench, takes off his jersey, and throws it at me.

"I hope you're happy," he says. "We could've won this game. I would've been just fine out there. Now I'm done! This team is done! *You and I* are done! I trusted you to keep your mouth shut. Now my mom is going to freak out and haul me into the doctor and get a huge bill she can't pay. If you could have just shut up I would've been fine in a couple days. I can take care of myself. I don't need you talking about me behind my back!"

"I'm sorry," I say. I don't know how else to explain to him that in my gut I knew he wasn't going to be okay if he played again. I don't know how to tell him that I wasn't going behind his back, but that I *had* his back. I promised his mother I'd watch out for him. I promised *myself*.

Anton gathers up his clothes and slams his locker shut.

When he's gone, I gear up and join the other guys out on the field, but there is a huge hole out there without Anton. I try to fill it by working twice as hard and getting the rest of the team pumped up, but I know it isn't enough.

Chapter 31

After Friday's playoff game, I stare out the car window as my dad drives us home. I replay the game in my head. I keep going over every mistake I made. I missed a block in the third quarter that let the Hornets get a touchdown, and without a real quarterback, we could barely move down the field. We lost 24–3 and I'm glad Anton wasn't there to see it.

"You played a tough game tonight," my dad says. "But you looked good out there. You looked strong. You've grown a lot since last year."

I just nod my head at this. I feel bad that he

missed work and drove through the night to just watch our team lose.

"Next year," he says.

"There's not going to be a next year," I say too fast. Too loud.

"You aren't giving up," my dad says looking over at me. "You love the game."

"This town is giving up on us," I say.

My dad has heard the news. I see him grip the steering wheel and stare straight ahead.

"Not everyone has given up," he says. "Your great-grandfather helped build that school. I'm not going to just watch them shut it down."

"There's no money to pay for all the repairs and keep it open."

My dad looks over at me and then back at the road.

"When the mine closed down, it left a hole in this town. It sucked a lot of hope and pride out this place. I'm not going to let it take anything more. The mine owes this town something. They owe us at least some money to repair our schools. I'm going to make some calls when we get home. We can put pressure on the company. I'm not giving up without a fight. If the mines won't step up and take action, I will."

I look over at my dad. I can see the determination in his face. It replaces the tired look that was there just a few minutes ago. I know he'll do everything he can do to keep the doors of Warren High open. He's never been one to back away from a challenge.

When we are almost home, I ask my dad to drop me off at Anton's house.

"Tell him about our plan," my dad says as I get out of the car. "Let him know I'm going to make some calls and gather up a bunch of us who used to work in the mines."

"Thanks," I say to my dad. "And thanks for driving all night to watch my game. Thanks for working so hard for Mom and me."

"Things will get better," my dad says. "We just have to keep doing the best we can until they do."

I give him a wave as he drives away, and then I climb up Anton's porch steps and knock softly on the front door.

His mom answers and hugs me. Anton's concussion was worse than any of us knew. When his mom took him to the ER, the doctor gave him a CAT scan and found bleeding in his brain. He was hospitalized for three days. Now he's back home and he's going to be okay, but he can't go back to school for another two weeks.

"Hey," I say as I enter Anton's dark room.

The foil balloons Ciara and I brought to the hospital are half-floating above his bed.

"What was the score?" he asks. He's not allowed to text or watch TV or be on a computer of any kind. *Complete brain rest*, his mother calls it.

"24–3," I answer.

He winces at this.

"Who played QB?"

"Joe Warner," I say. "That really skinny freshman," I remind him. Anton nods at this.

"How did he not get crushed?"

"We built a wall around the kid," I say "And he managed to make a couple of nice passes."

"Did Coach chew through an entire pack of gum?" Anton asks.

"I think he was on his third pack by the third quarter," I say.

Anton smiles at this.

I pull up a chair and sit next to him.

"My dad is going to see if he can get some money from the mines to keep Warren High open."

"Yeah," Anton says sitting up in his bed. "That's a good idea. We should all write letters to the CEO. Every student. Every person in this town. Maybe get the press involved. "

I see him wince.

"Don't think so much," I say.

He looks at me and says, "The problem is, I didn't think enough. I'm sorry, Busby. I'm sorry for blaming you."

"You didn't know how bad it was," I say.

"Now I do," he says. He looks over at me. "Thanks for watching out for me. You had my back."

I'm embarrassed by this. Every time Anton and his mother thank me for what I did, I go bright red. The truth is, I could've done more—and I could've done it earlier. I'm just glad Anton's going to be okay. "Rest up. We need you to get better."

"I will," he replies. "I really will this time." And I can tell he means it.

"Good," I smile. "Because next year, we take the field again."

"Yeah," he says, but he says it in a distant way, and I realize that neither one of us can predict what will happen next year. We can only keep moving forward and watching out for each other and helping each other up when one of us takes a hit.

"Stop by tomorrow," he says.

"I will," I say. "Maybe I can tell you about the game."

"Good," he says. "Good."

He closes his eyes, and I let him rest.

Check out all
the GRIDIRON Books

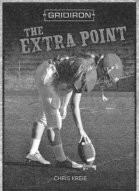

Leave it all on the field!

K.R. Coleman is a writer, teacher, and parent of two boys. Coleman can often be found jotting down ideas in a notebook while watching a hockey or baseball game or while walking along the many trails that encircle Minneapolis. Currently, Coleman teaches at the Loft Literary Center and is working on a young adult novel entitled *Air*.